Published 2015 by Geddes & Grosset, an imprint of The Gresham
Publishing Company Ltd, Academy Park, Building 4000,
Gower Street, Glasgow, G51 1PR, Scotland

Copyright © 1996 The Gresham Publishing Company Ltd
Endpaper images copyright © Attitude, courtesy of Shutterstock

All rights reserved. No part of this publication may be reproduced,
stored in a retrieval system or transmitted in any form or by
any means, electronic, mechanical, photocopying, recording or
otherwise, without the prior permission of the copyright holder.

Conditions of Sale:
This book is sold with the condition that it will not, by way of trade
or otherwise, be resold, hired out, lent, or otherwise distributed or
circulated in any form or style of binding or cover other than that
in which it is published and without the same conditions being
imposed on the subsequent purchaser.

ISBN 978-1-910680-68-1

Printed and bound in Malaysia

4 5 6 7 8 9 10

On the Move

Judy Hamilton
Illustrated by Mimi Everett

Tarantula
EARLY LEARNERS

James is walking.

Jemma crawls on her hands and knees.

Alan has a wheelchair to help him to get about.

The twins are being pushed along in their buggy.

They are all on the move. In what other ways can we get on the move?

Cycles are a great way to get on the move!
They come in all sizes:

Cycles can have three wheels,

or two wheels,

Or even just one wheel!

Charlie has a motorcycle. It has not got pedals. It has a powerful engine to make it move.

How about a car to get you on the move? This family needs a big car to hold Mum, Dad, three children, a dog and lots of luggage!

Cars come in all sorts of shapes and sizes:

Some cars are made to go very fast indeed — look at this racing car!

Get on the move by bus!
Buses have room for lots of people.
Buses can help you to move about town,
or they can take you travelling to faraway
places.

This bus has got an upstairs and a downstairs. It is a double-decker bus.

This bus is a single-decker bus.

Look at all the lorries! They have lots of room in them for moving all sorts of things from place to place. Can you guess what some of them are carrying?

Some lorries are specially built with tanks on the back for carrying liquids, like petrol. They are called tankers.

This lorry is a transporter. It carries cars from the factory to the showroom.

Some people need to get on the move to help other people. They have vehicles that are made specially for them.

This ambulance has plenty of room in it for sick or injured people. The ambulance driver can drive them quickly and safely to hospital.

Fire engines need plenty of room for all the fire fighters as well as their ladders and hoses.

Police cars need to move very fast when they are speeding to an emergency.

Many people need to be on the move when they are working.

The postman needs a van to help him to deliver parcels all around town.

The milkman has a milk float to help him to carry all the milk to the houses.

The farmer has a tractor to help him with his work on the farm.

And this boy uses his roller skates to speed up his paper round!

It's fun to be on the move in a train! Railway stations are busy places, full of excitement.

Trains can carry all sorts of things — people, letters and parcels, goods and machinery.

Some cities have special trains that travel underground, speeding through long tunnels far below the streets.

How about getting on the move in the water?
You could skim across the waves in a yacht,

sail the ocean blue in a cruise ship,

paddle a canoe,

or row a rowing boat!

Hovercrafts can travel fast across the water. So can speedboats. Which one will win?

Leave the earth far behind and get on the move in the air!
You could fly in a great big aeroplane,

or a little one.

How about a hot air balloon?

Space rockets travel farthest of all above the earth. Next stop the Moon!

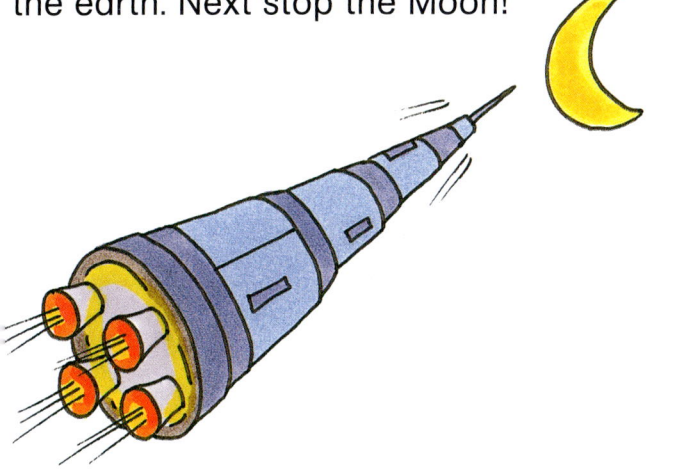

Long ago, before engines were invented, people used horses to get them on the move. You can still do this today.
You could ride a horse like this one:

You could drive in a little cart like this:

Or you might like to sit in a stately carriage like this one!

Getting on the move can be fun! Look at this picture and try to count all the different ways of getting on the move that you can see.

How do you like to get on the move?